D0602226

Summer Jackson
★ Grown Up ★

By Teresa E. Harris Illustrated by AG Ford

KATHERINE TEGEN BOOKS
An Imprint of HarperCollins Publishers

Katherine Tegen Books is an imprint of HarperCollins Publishers.

Summer Jackson: Grown Up

Text copyright © 2011 by Teresa E. Harris

Illustrations copyright © 2011 by AG Ford

Library of Congress Cataloging-in-Publication Data is available.
ISBN 978-0-06-185757-7 (trade bdg.) — ISBN 978-0-06-185758-4 (lib. bdg.)

Typography by Rachel Zegar
11 12 13 14 15 SCP 10 9 8 7 6 5 4 3 2 1
❖
First Edition

For Bria,
the original Summer Jackson
—T.H.

To my little cousins,
nieces, and nephews
—A.F.

My name is Summer Jackson
and I'm tired of being seven.
Two scoops of ice cream are *not* enough.
Hand puppets are *not* that funny.
And eight o'clock is *way* too early for bed.

My mama and daddy say I can be anything I want to be when I grow up.

I can be a truck driver,

a lawyer,

or a juggler in the circus.

I can even be a huge ginger cat with a black spot on my nose—but only on Halloween.

But I don't want to be any of those things. I just want to be a grown-up— **starting right now.**

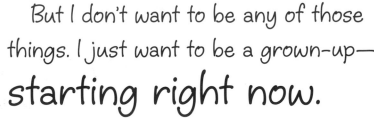

From now on, I will wear very high heels with very pointy toes.

And maybe a blazer.

I'll get a cell phone. It will ring all the time.

And I'll wear sunglasses—everywhere.

I show Mama and Daddy my new look.
"From here on out, I am Summer Jackson, Grown Up."

In the morning, I read the newspaper over breakfast.

At school I eat my lunch with a knife and fork,

and during recess I make a to-do list.

At night Daddy lets me watch TV with him and Mama. We watch the twenty-four-hour news network, and when someone says something I don't like, I say, "That's preposterous!" and shake my fist at the television.

Everyone knows that grown-ups have grown-up jobs—even Mama and Daddy. Daddy wears a suit to work every day and bosses people around. Mama is a consultant. She says this means that people pay her to make decisions for them.

I think I'll be a big-time consultant, too.
That's why I'm carrying this briefcase.

I meet with my clients during playtime.

"So, what you're saying is you want to play soccer during recess, but you want to play basketball, and you want to poke bugs with a stick? Okay. Monday and Wednesday, soccer; Tuesday and Thursday, basketball; and on Fridays you poke bugs with a stick. Get it? Got it? Good. That will be $2.50."

"Summer, what do you think you're doing?"

When did Principal Cutter get here?
"Call me Miss Jackson, if you please," I tell her.

Principal Cutter calls Mama and Daddy. When I
get home from school, they sit me down for a talk.
"Taking money from your classmates?"
"Don't you think this has gone on long enough?"
"Doesn't anyone play tag anymore?"

"I have to take this."

Mama and Daddy follow me to my room. They just walk right in!

"Summer," Mama says, "we've talked things over and we think you should be able to be as grown up as you like—starting right now."

I'm so happy Mama is being a grown-up herself.

Mama makes hamburgers for dinner.
"I was really hoping for pâté," I tell her.

Mama says, "One order of
hamburger paste coming right up!"

Wait, one order of *what*?!

I think I'll just eat my green beans instead.

When Mama and Daddy finish eating, they get right up. They don't move their plates or anything! "Who's going to clear the table?" I ask.

Mama and Daddy shrug.

"*Someone* has to do it or else we'll get ants."

"I think we'll leave it to the grown-up," Daddy says.

"But—"

I really don't like ants. So I clear off the dinner table and put the dishes in the sink. This isn't fair. I'm just a— grown-up! That's what I am.

And grown-ups should get to eat as much ice cream for dessert as they like. One scoop, two, three, four, and . . .

Oh, I don't feel so well. Maybe it's time for bed.

But Mama and Daddy are in my room, in my bed.
"We got scared of the dark. We need to sleep with
a grown-up," Daddy says.
   "My bed isn't big enough for all of us!"
   "Sure it is," Mama says. "Hop in."

After breakfast Mama says, "Your father and I are going outside to play in the backyard. Do you want to play with us?"

"No. Not today. I have to—"

"Weeeee!"

Daddy's pushing Mama on the swing. "Yippee!"

Mama pushes Daddy down the slide. They sure sound like they're having a lot of fun. Maybe I'll go outside, just to get a closer look. . . .

And maybe I'll go down the slide, just once.

And it's all right if Daddy pushes me on the swing, just for a little while. Before I know it, I'm swinging higher and higher.

Then I jump off, and Mama and Daddy chase me around the yard.
"You're it!"
"No, you're it!"

We fall down in a giggly, out-of-breath heap.

"We love you," Mama says.

"No matter if you want to be seven—or seventy," Daddy says.

"Well, I guess I'll be seven, but I'll still wear
my sunglasses—everywhere—and—"
"You'll help with the breakfast dishes?"

"I have to take this."